Here's what people have to say about the Jannah Jewels Adventure Book Series:

I can't continue without saying it one more time: Powerful Young Muslim Girls! No damsels in distress, no dominating male protagonist, no cliché girly nonsense! ... This is exactly what our girls need to grow up reading.
–Emma Apple, author-illustrator of best-selling 'Children's First Questions' Series

Learning about Islamic history and famous Muslims of the past makes these books a historical book lover's wish, and the Islamic twist is a plus for young Muslim readers. Jannah Jewels has been Muslimommy approved as kid-friendly!
-Zakiyya Osman, MusliMommy.com

I love all of the Jannah Jewels books, and the fact that you combine history and adventure in your stories. I also liked that you put the holy verses of Quran that remind us to stay close to Allah and I liked the fact that in one book you mentioned the verse from Quran which mentions the benefit of being kind to your enemy. I have read all of the Jannah Jewels books and even read two of these books in one day, that's how much I like these books!
–Fatima Bint Saifurrehman, 8 Years Old

I could really feel the love that went into this book – the characters, the places, the history, and the things that the author clearly strongly believes in and wants to share with our children and the wider world through her heroines...My daughter's verdict? "I would give the book a 10 out of 10 mum"
–Umm Salihah, HappyMuslimah.com Blog

Fantastic book! My child was turning pages and couldn't wait to read the next chapter. So much so he's asking for the next book ...
-Mrs. S. A. Khanom, Book Reviewer

By Umm Nura

Vancouver

This book is dedicated to my three little Jannah Jewels,
Nura, Hanaan and Hakim.

Published by Gentle Breeze Books, Vancouver, B.C., Canada

Copyright 2013 by Umm Nura
Illustrations by Nayzak Al-Hilali

Visit us on the Web! www.JannahJewels.com

ISBN: 978-0-9867208-5-7

September 2013

Contents

Sport:

Archery

Role:

Guides and leads the girls

Superpower:

Intense sight and spiritual insight

Fear:

Spiders

Special Gadget:

Ancient Compass

Carries:

Bow and Arrow, Ancient Map, Compass

HIDAYAH

JAIDE

Sport:

Skateboarding

Role:

Artist, Racer

Superpower:

Fast racer on foot or skateboard

Fear:

Hunger (She's always hungry!)

Special Gadget:

Time Travel Watch

Carries:

Skateboard, Sketchpad, Pencil, Watch

Sport:

Horseback Riding

Role:

Walking Encyclopedia,
Horseback Rider

Superpower:

Communicates with
animals

Fear:

Heights

Special Gadget:

Book of Knowledge

Carries:

Book of Knowledge, has
horse named "Spirit"

IMAN

SARA

Sport:

Swimming

Role:

Environmentalist,
Swimmer

Superpower:

Breathes underwater for
a long time

Fear:

Drowning

Special Gadget:

Metal Ball

Carries:

Sunscreen, Water
canteen, Metal Ball

SUPPORTING CHARACTERS

JAFFAR

AL-KINDI

BANU MUSA BROTHERS

MASTER ARTIST

THE JANNAH JEWELS ADVENTURE 3:

Baghdad, Iraq

ARTIFACT 3: SCROLL PEN IN BAGHDAD

"Hit the target with your heart."
~Sensei to Hidayah

Dear Reader, Assalamu'alaykum,

What an adventure in China!

The Jannah Jewels struggled with fiery arrows, an angry Jaffar and a windy storm! They met the great admiral Zheng He who helped the Jannah Jewels with his mighty ship and amazing crew.

Sara showed great skill in the ocean waters and the Jannah Jewels found the missing artifact!

Now, the mystery turns to the wondrous city of Baghdad. Here, they will be faced with an even angrier Jaffar who brings his friends to help him find the missing artifact before Hidayah!

Come along, dear Reader, and help the Jannah Jewels find the missing artifact in Book 3, Bravery in Baghdad.

May Peace be with you,
Umm Nura

Prologue

Learning archery was Hidayah's favorite part of the day. She looked forward to the time when she could hold her magnificent bow and arrow and be with her friends at the dojo. Hidayah was orphaned at a young age and the students of the dojo soon became like family to her. Likewise, the Sensei started to become a lot like a mother to Hidayah. Hidayah also spent much of her time with three of her closest companions Iman, Sara and Jaide, who altogether called themselves the Jannah Jewels.

Hidayah led a pretty simple life up until that fateful day she spotted those long red flowing robes floating up to the empty house on the hill. Ever since that day, Hidayah's life was never the same.

Training with the Sensei wasn't easy. Hidayah had to wake up with the rooster and jog up the gigantic rocky hill before her eyes could even crack open. The Sensei wanted to practice early in the morning as she advised that this was the best time to do things, right after Fajr, the pre-dawn prayer.

The Sensei had turned her living room into a dojo. There was a large open space and huge vertical mirrors covering one wall. There were several lanterns hanging from the ceiling by hooks, their light casting a warm glow in the carpet-less dojo.

On the other side of the wall was one large square window that looked onto the Sensei's herb garden and a cluster of maple trees just like the time-travel tree in the neighborhood park. Hidayah started to take regular archery lessons with the Sensei and it was not long after that Hidayah proved to be a natural archer. In turn, the Sensei gave Hidayah extra special attention because she recognized her gift. Hidayah also had to train extra long hours so she could work towards mastery.

"Mastery of archery is very important," said the Sensei. "You don't just learn the basics and think you know everything. You have to practice every day and become so skilled that you could shoot an arrow with your eyes closed."

"There are four main areas of archery, Hidayah. Of course, there is the physical part. You have to train your muscles to hold the bow. It is heavier than you think. In the second area of archery, you have to train yourself to "still" your mind because you are worried often.

"How can I not be, Sensei? The state of the world is in chaos and we need peace to quickly return. The Peaceful Archer passed away and has left this enormous task upon my shoulders," said Hidayah.

"Precisely why you need to practice deep breathing, too," said the Sensei. "Then, there is the spiritual part of the archery training, which means you need to serve others."

Everyone was given a special role in the dojo to help them understand the importance of giving to others before oneself. Some students tended to the garden, some swept the floors, some lit the lanterns and some worked in the dojo's library. All of the roles were significant, each teaching a certain lesson to the student.

Hidayah's service to others was learning to make and serve brilliant mint green tea for all the people who came to the dojo. There was much wisdom to be learnt in making green tea, her Sensei said, and even more wisdom to be gained through serving it to others.

"The final part of the archery training is to keep a strong connection with God and His Messenger, peace and blessings be upon him, at all times," said the Sensei.

This was probably the part of the training that was the most difficult for Hidayah. She had to have a clear heart and remember her roots often. Or else Sensei would seem like she was talking in riddles when she would share her wisdom; and sometimes Hidayah didn't understand her teacher at all!

"It's not about hitting the target, it's about your aim and your heart," said the Sensei.

So you don't want me to hit the target?

"Hit the target with your heart."

You mean I don't use my arrows?

"You are the target and the arrow."

What? How can I be the target and the arrow?

The Sensei wouldn't talk much about where she came from, her family or why she seemed to live alone.

"In time, things will reveal themselves to you. *Sabr* Hidayah, *Patience*," the Sensei would say.

Hidayah kept asking the Sensei questions anyway,

to which she received answers in silence or in smiles. Never did the Sensei show any agitation at the questions being asked. She was always patient, always ready to listen.

Hidayah sat in the window bench that looked out on Sensei's herb garden. She watched her friends who were busy weeding and tending the soil. She closed her eyes and rested her head against the wall. She let herself be taken back into an earlier memory she kept close to her heart.

It was morning and Hidayah woke up early and jogged up the hill to meet her Sensei. Little did she know, it would be a day she would never forget. Hidayah entered the dojo and joined the other students already there, sitting on their knees with their legs beneath them. They sat motionless, while the Sensei began reciting the opening chapter of the Qur'an, the Fatihah:

In the Name of God,
the Most Merciful, the Most Compassionate
Praise be to God
Lord Sustainer of the Worlds

The Most Merciful, the Most Compassionate

Master of the Day of Reckoning

You Alone do we worship

And to You Alone we turn in need

Guide us along the road straight

The road of those whom You have blessed

Not those with anger upon them

Not those who have lost the way.

Amen

Each of the students recited melodiously after her, line after line, finally ending with 'amen' that filled the walls of the dojo. The first break of sunlight poured into the dojo as it rose in the morning sky. The light of the sun bounced off the high vertical mirrors the Sensei had placed on one wall. Light filled the home with brilliance. The girls took their stances standing all in a row side by side. Each student was given their bows and arrows. The Sensei walked around and adjusted one girl this way and another that way. It had been months already and nobody was allowed to shoot the arrow, yet. The Sensei said that the students were just not ready.

Some students left out of frustration at not being allowed to shoot the arrow.

"Impatience is not a mark of a true archer," said the Sensei. "You need timing, accuracy and patience to shoot well."

The remaining students worked hard on all of the four areas with diligence: body, mind, spirit and heart. They relearned how to hold the bow and arrow with respect and grace and practiced their deep breathing and centering of the heart. The students had to show a certain kind of "inner wisdom" before they would ever be allowed to actually shoot the arrow. The time had finally come.

Hidayah walked into the kitchen during break time and immediately started to make the brilliant mint green tea. She started with the loose tea leaves, placing them inside a beautiful pot with a long arched spout. She boiled some water in a separate whistling kettle and then poured it carefully on top of the green leaves. The aroma of the green tea filled the air as the first heat of the water touched the leaves. She carefully watched the water change from a dark yellow to a brilliant yellow.

She waited a certain while and then gathered some mint leaves from the herb garden. She washed and trimmed the mint leaves and then placed them into the pot. Another lovely scent filled the air. She then let the tea sit for another certain while. Then she placed a spoon of honey into each clear glass just the way her Sensei had taught her. She lifted the tea-pot high in the air and poured the tea into each glass. The arch of the tea matched the arch of the spout on the pot. Tea-making was an Art and Hidayah had mastered it.

Honey was a very important part of the tea-making. The Sensei mentioned that it was so important that God mentioned honey in the Holy Book. Prophet Muhammad, peace and blessings be upon him, also explained how to use honey for good health.

Hidayah loved the sweet honey aroma that filled the walls of the dojo. She placed all the glasses onto a tray and began to walk over to each student. She made sure that her Sensei received the first glass.

"JazakiAllah khair, Hidayah, thank you," said the Sensei. She held up the clear glass to examine the color against the sunlight, giving Hidayah a reassuring, 'well done' nod. Hidayah walked over to each of her companions and handed them a glass of tea which they drank in silence while watching the Sensei with eagerness.

All of a sudden, the Sensei rose to her feet in one grand movement, her red robes flowing around her. Her eyes were intense and her posture straight and confident.

"It is time to shoot the first arrow," said the Sensei.

Everybody gasped.

"Hidayah will be first," she said. "Everybody outside, please."

"I - I didn't practice today. I was making the tea. I'm not ready," stammered Hidayah.

"You did practice today. Tea-making has a lot to do with the bow and arrow, Hidayah. The grace, stillness, focus and patience it takes to make the tea all matter in archery. You have served your companions for months and have mastered strength and gentleness in the way that you serve. You are ready, trust me," said the Sensei.

Hidayah's hands became sweaty. Her face felt hot

and her head dizzy. She gently set down the tray of tea-cups and picked up her long bamboo bow from her teacher. Everybody gathered outside, whispering to each other that Hidayah would be first!

"Look to the target with your heart of service and you will always reach your goal," said the Sensei.

Hidayah pulled back on the string, her hands hurting a bit from the stretch. She closed one eye...

"No, no, you keep both eyes open, Hidayah," said the Sensei.

Hidayah opened her eyes again.

When Hidayah stretched the string of the bow back, it formed a perfect circle. The arrow sat in the bow parallel to the ground, level with her heart. She breathed in and then as she breathed out, she released the arrow!

The long sharp arrow glided through the still air, making a whirring sound as it flew past and quickly gained speed. Hidayah stayed motionless, saying a quiet prayer in her heart. The arrow surged forward, as if on a mission of its own, strong, courageous, and fierce.

"Thwamp!"

Everybody gasped.

The arrow had landed right in the middle of the target!

The Sensei smiled a knowing smile. Hidayah blushed.

"SubhanAllah, I can't believe it!" she said.

Her companions cheered!

"You didn't do anything, Hidayah. It is God who did it for you. Do you remember the story of the Messenger of God, peace and blessings be upon him, when he threw a handful of dust and defeated those who wished to harm him by it? God revealed to His Messenger this wisdom:

"When you threw (a handful of dust), it was not you who threw it, but God Himself who did, in order that He might test the Believers by a gracious trial from Himself: for God is He Who hears and knows all things.

Indeed, Hidayah remembered the story, it was one of her favorites. But she had never realized such a gracious thing could happen to her, in a way, too.

With Hidayah's first arrow, the Sensei and Hidayah forged a deeper bond of teacher and student, and now Hidayah practiced with renewed fortitude and patience.

"Stand with your head held high," said the Sensei. "Don't slouch. Relax in your shoulders! Remember to breathe and aim with your heart, not only with your eyes."

After class, all the students left talking about Hidayah and her great ability.

On that same special day, the Sensei revealed a special technique to help focus Hidayah's heart before she let go of the arrow.

"Place your hand on top of her heart and feel the beat," she said.

Hidayah watched her Sensei do this every time she let go of the arrow; there was this brief moment where she would connect with her heart. After awhile, the Sensei would simply gaze down at her heart, not even looking at the target. Hidayah practiced this technique of focusing on her heart for months and it really helped.

*　　　*　　　*　　　*　　　*　　　*　　　*

"Hidayah! Hidayah!" called Jaide. "Where are you?"

"There she is," said Iman. "On the window bench."

Hidayah snapped out of her daydream.

"Listen up girls, the Sensei wants to tell us about our next mission!" said Iman.

The girls all entered the dojo and sat on their knees in front of the Sensei.

"Jannah Jewels, you will be travelling back into time to Baghdad. You will visit the most wondrous building of the time. Someone is in grave danger there. You must work together, find the 3rd artifact for the Golden Clock - and, do so quickly, before time runs out!"

The Jannah Jewels closed their eyes and joined hands. *Could Hidayah find the artifact, save a person from danger, and return back home with the Jannah Jewels? What Hidayah really wondered was if she was truly ready to meet the angry Jaffar.*

1

Jaffar And Jasmin

Sitting with her brother in the large living room of their family's home, Jasmin attempted to nurse Jaffar's bleeding wounds. His hand was swollen from his last encounter with the Jannah Jewels in China.

"Don't touch me, Jasmin," said Jaffar.

"Oh c'mon, Jaffar, let me help you. I feel bad. You are so stressed out about seeing Father!" said Jasmin.

"I don't trust you, Jasmin," said Jaffar. "How can I? You kept such a huge secret from me!"

"Well, then, don't trust me," said Jasmin, sitting down and sulking. "Here he comes!"

"Peace be upon you, my children," Khan greeted Jasmin and Jaffar as he walked into the room.

15

"And upon you be peace and God's Mercy, dear Father," replied Jaffar and Jasmin.

"A word please, Jaffar. Jasmin, go, run along," said Khan.

"Can I please stay, Father, puh-lease? I am worried about the world too, you know!" said Jasmin.

"No," was the simple answer from her father.

Jasmin silently walked to the door of the room, wishing with all her heart she could stay for what she knew would be an important conversation.

Jaffar moved himself up on the red velvet sofa and balanced his hand on the armrest.

What now, another scolding for losing another artifact? thought Jaffar.

"How are you feeling?" asked Khan.

"Alhamdulillah. Fine, I guess, a little nauseous," said Jaffar.

"Well, you better get over it. The next mission is here and this time you won't fail! Jasmin doesn't know this yet but I'm sending her with you! You obviously need help. Time is running out for the next Master Archer to emerge and I need the secret in the Golden Clock; I need the secret NOW," said Khan.

"No, no, you can't send Jasmin! I have Moe and Slim with me. They will help me," said Jaffar.

"Moe and Slim? Hahaha! Those two annoying friends of yours can't do anything! Haha! You can't be serious?" said Khan.

Jasmin listened on, from where she stood just behind the door of the room. She was excited at the thought of time-travel! It's what she dreamed about!

"I need one more chance, Father, one more chance. Jasmin is too young; she can't help me. She's always getting into trouble and she'll only get me into trouble too. Send Moe and Slim with me and I will show you victory," said Jaffar.

Khan thought for a moment and then boomed "ONE LAST CHANCE, Jaffar! I might send just Jasmin and not you at all! Don't you know what this means to me, to our family, to your mother if she were here to see it? You need to bring back the honour to me, the obvious heir to the throne after the Master Archer. You must win back the artifacts and find the secret in the Golden Clock."

"I'm trying! I need Moe and Slim. Hidayah has help, she has the Jannah Jewels with her!" said Jaffar.

"Have you even located the Golden Clock yet?" asked Khan.

"No, but I saw the ancient compass; Hidayah has it. It seems to guide Hidayah to the artifacts and back to the Golden Clock. I have a feeling it is close by. I have to find a way to follow her back through her time travel machine," said Jaffar.

"GO! If we can intercept the artifacts, then Hidayah will have to show us the Golden Clock anyway. Either find the Clock or get the artifacts or *both*!"

"Yeah right!" said Jasmin from behind the door.

"Jasmin!" boomed Khan and Jaffar.

Jasmin laughed down the hall while Jaffar fell back onto the sofa from exhaustion. Khan left while Jaffar gazed out the window. He thought back to China. He wondered why Hidayah would help him when he was drowning in the ocean while she was on Zheng He's ship. He shook his head trying to make sense of it. Still, Jaffar knew he had to defeat her!

Jaffar bandaged up his arm and put on his boots. He peered over the map his father had left him at the end of their conversation about his next mission. It was a draft copy that Khan's assistant had found in the Peaceful Archer's library.

Jaffar began pacing up and down the room. He was furious that he hadn't been able to return from China with the second artifact - the medicinal plant from Southeast Asia. The Jannah Jewels had outwitted him yet again!

Another thought went through his soul, much deeper: *I can't believe I thought mother was dead. Where is she? Now, it's just me and Father and pesky Jasmin. Mother would know what to do if she were here.*

Jaffar was determined to find the secret before Hidayah. He wanted to prove once and for all to his father that he was a great archer, despite what his father believed. Jaffar's anger fueled him to continue this search. His anger was both his victory and his downfall. He was still working on how to control it. If he didn't get so angry, then he wouldn't have burned his hand in the Ring of Fire in China.

Jaffar sat down and looked at a map.

"Jaffar, you can do this," said an old man's voice.

Jaffar turned around.

"Uncle Idrees!" said Jaffar.

Jaffar hugged him tightly. Jaffar was flooded with feelings of relief.

"I heard about what was happening and I came as soon as I could," said Uncle Idrees.

Uncle Idrees was Khan's brother. He was a short, funny man with a long thin white beard who laughed a lot. He wore a white cap on his head that always appeared a bit too small for his head. He was known to be very wise and highly-skilled in archery.

"Does Father know you are here?" asked Jaffar. "He won't be happy to see you."

"I know, that's why I came to see you first! Hahaha! Now where are those friends of yours?" said Uncle Idrees. "We have a mystery to solve. Hahaha!"

2

The House of Wisdom

"In the Name of God, Most Beneficent, Most Merciful!" said the Jannah Jewels.

As they opened their eyes, they quickly found out that they were standing on top of a steep hill *but not for long!* Jaide dropped her skateboard and hopped on.

"Oh no you don't. I am not getting on that thing!" said Iman.

"We'll just meet you at the bottom then," said Jaide. "Who knows where we are and what danger awaits us."

"Oh alright, alright, I'm just not sitting in the front," said Iman.

The Jannah Jewels all crowded on top of Jaide's skateboard and off they flew. The girls went swooping

down, narrowly missing branches and bushes. They could see an ancient building surrounded by some people, at the bottom of the hill. The building looked stunning in the beaming sunlight.

The Jannah Jewels, crouching together on the skateboard, were quickly gaining speed; the wind rushed past them, whipping across their faces. Fear and panic started filling Iman, who was terribly afraid of heights "Somebody better do something, RIGHT NOW!" screamed Iman.

If I could just reach back a little bit more and grab the bow and arrow, thought Hidayah.

She tried to keep her face straight, so the wind would not attack her. She twisted her arm back.

I'm glad I took those strength-training classes even though they were on Saturday morning, thought Hidayah.

"Got it!" she cried.

The skateboard raced on forward. The girls held on to each other tightly as they whizzed through the air. Iman tried to pull back, like she was riding a horse. The large group of people gathered at the foot of the hill looked up, shielding their eyes from the sun. Suddenly, the crowd gasped as Jaide stood tall, balancing herself on the skateboard.

"Piece of cake," said Jaide, riding her skateboard like a champion.

Hidayah slowly stood up too. Jaide held Hidayah by the waist as she attached a rope to an arrow and quickly shot it into a tree they just passed by. It landed straight inside the trunk. The long rope was in the tree and the other end was in Hidayah's hands.

"Everybody hold on!" she cried.

Jaide grabbed the rope and the Jannah Jewels held on with all their might. All of a sudden, Sara lost grip of the rope and then Iman, Jaide and Hidayah too! The Jannah Jewels were falling, legs were scrambling, Iman was shrieking. Down down down they went!

SPLASH!

The Jannah Jewels landed in a large fountain in the middle of a courtyard. One by one, their heads bobbed up out of the water, their hijabs stuck to them like glue from being completely soaked. Hands reached out to them, to pull them out of the fountain. Then, a young man wearing long white robes and a matching white turban emerged and with authority, bid the rest of the spectators away.

He addressed the girls, now standing in puddles in front of the fountain, "You must be the Jannah Jewels? You're a lot smaller than what I expected."

"Why does everyone keep saying that about us?" said Jaide under her breath.

"I am al-Kindi. I was studying in the Bayt-al-Hikma just now when I saw you from the windows," he continued. "This is the most beautiful library of Baghdad. Welcome."

"Baghdad?!" exclaimed Sara. "We're in Iraq! That means this beautiful building in front of us is... is... the incredible House of Wisdom! SubhanAllah, I can't believe it!"

"You are al-Kindi! You've translated a lot of books from Greek into Arabic," said Iman. "You've studied so many subjects such as medicine, optics, mathematics, and astronomy. I've always wondered what you were like, I've read about you in 'Famous Inventors Week' at school."

"SubhanAllah! I am still researching and studying many of those things right now," said al-Kindi. "Welcome to the 9th century!"

"Thank goodness we are not in the 13th century," said Sara.

"What was that?" asked al-Kindi, with curiosity in his voice.

"Uh, umm, nothing," stammered Sara. She turned to Iman. "We are still hundreds of years away from the horrendous Mongol Invasion," whispered Sara. "We can't let al-Kindi know, he'll feel sad about what is to happen to this beautiful place."

"The Mongol Invasion?" asked Jaide.

"Ssshhh! Not so loud," snapped Sara.

"They did awful things," whispered Iman. "They threw all the books of knowledge from the great library into the Tigris River! The people that survived said that the Tigris River ran black for over six months from the ink of the scholars - from the books they wrote," whispered Hidayah.

"I'm glad we're not in that year!" said Jaide loudly.

"What was that?" asked al-Kindi. "What year, what are you talking about?" Al-Kindi's long white robes and white turban made his brown eyes shine brightly.

"Uh, nothing, nothing. Not year — uh ear, yeah ear! I'm glad I don't have anything in my ear!" stammered Jaide.

Hidayah and Sara both rolled their eyes at Jaide. Jaide pulled on her hoodie to hide her blushing face.

"Anyway, there is no time to lose. Let me show you the Bayt-al-Hikma, the House of Wisdom, and tell you what happened. We've been waiting for you. We need your help."

3

The Missing Son

The Jannah Jewels followed behind al-Kindi as they entered an enormous library filled with people peering over books, some discussing notes in small circles, some writing with long pens and bottles of ink and others talking excitedly with their hands.

All the girls were speechless. They didn't know such a place even existed, especially in the 9th century. They had entered what is known in the world today as the Golden Age of Islam. Scientists, inventors, mathematicians, poets and scholars from all over the world shared knowledge with each other, translating books into different languages.

"This... is... the House of Wisdom," gasped Hidayah,

looking all around. "This is truly amazing!"

Iman was standing on a chair on her tiptoes looking at manuscripts on the top shelf, just like they did back in Timbuktu in Mali. The girls had to drag her out of the main hall as they were lead to a small room with a large table and chairs. The girls sat down on the edges of their seats.

"The son of one of our translators has been kidnapped," al-Kindi explained. "His name is Ishaq. He was sent on a mission by my colleague al-Khawarizmi, to find a valuable and rare book in a nearby village and bring it back here to add to the collection. Ishaq reached there safely and got the book. He sent a messenger pigeon to tell us that he was on his way back, but..." his voice trailed off.

"Oh no," said Sara.

"He has not returned. We think someone took Ishaq because of the valuable book he has in his possession," said al-Kindi.

"The next missing artifact for the Golden Clock must be the book that Ishaq has," said Jaide. "When we find Ishaq, we'll find the artifact too."

Hidayah pulled the tight cork from her bamboo container with a pop. She had made the container out of bamboo, on their last mission, to keep the map of artifacts safe and dry. She took out the ancient map and unraveled it. Peering at the number three on the map, Hidayah noted that it was indeed beside Baghdad in Iraq, but that the artifact wasn't in the shape of a book.

"That's strange," said Hidayah. "The next artifact is not a book at all, it's a long pen, like the ones the scholars are using in the main hall."

"Hmmm, we should still try to help al-Kindi find Ishaq," said Sara. "It might lead us to the missing artifact."

"Yes, exactly, maybe the same people who have taken Ishaq for the book also know something about the pen," said Jaide drawing the pen from the map in her sketchbook. The pen was long and had a small round ball shape at its very top.

"What would be so important about a pen?" asked Sara.

"Well, I actually know the answer to something! I carry a special pen that I use to make my sketches.

To others it looks like any old artist pen, but to me it is valuable because it is mine," said Jaide. "The pen we are looking for probably belongs to a famous scholar here and would be worth a lot of money back home!"

Jaide passed around her favourite artist pen, showing al-Kindi and all the girls. It was a long black pen with a sharp triangular point at the end where the ink came out. Jaide drew beautiful art and calligraphy with it.

Al-Kindi took a closer look at the drawing. "You said it looks like the ones the scholars here are using, but it's slightly different - it's got a shape that I've never seen before. It might belong to one of the scholars who has travelled to the House of Wisdom from a foreign land. It's not one that is typical of Baghdad craftmanship. I'd say it's almost Indian in style. I'd have you check with my colleague Sind ibn Ali, who is from India and came to the House of Wisdom to work with us here, but he is away on an engineering project to assist our other colleague, al Farghani."

"Thank you for your help," said Hidayah. "And about Ishaq, could you tell us anything else that would be

31

important to his story?"

"Well, the last people to have seen Ishaq were the Banu Musa Brothers," said al-Kindi.

"Who are the Banu Musa Brothers and when can we talk to them?" asked Sara.

"The Banu Musa Brothers are three brothers who are amazing mathematicians, scientists and inventors. They are here, almost all the time, working on their devices," said al-Kindi. "Let's visit them in the stunning astronomy observatory."

The astronomy observatory in the House of Wisdom was used to study the stars, the moon, the sun and navigation. People used the lab to make calculations based on the positions of the stars in order to indicate changes in weather patterns, predict eclipses and chart the cycle of the seasons.

The Jannah Jewels entered a large room and sure enough the Banu Musa Brothers were there, huddled over a large drawing, talking in whispers.

4

The Ancient Compass

"Assalamu alaykum," said al-Kindi. "Here are the Jannah Jewels to help us find Ishaq." The girls repeated the greetings of peace.

"Walaikum asalaam wa Rahmatullah wa Barakatuh," said the Banu Musa Brothers.

"You are a lot smaller than we thought," said one brother.

"Here we go again," said Jaide. "Size has nothing to do with what we can do, Sir. This is our third mission. We have already found an ancient manuscript from the hot desert of Timbuktu and we escaped pirates, a fierce storm and flaming arrows in China too. We can solve this mystery!"

"Please excuse us all, we're all just feeling anxious about finding our friend," said al-Kindi. "Allow me to formally introduce the Banu Musa Brothers."

"Pleased to meet you!" said the Jannah Jewels.

"And we are pleased to make your acquaintance, Jannah Jewels. Any leads on Ishaq yet?" asked the eldest-looking brother.

"We are putting together the clues right now. We hear that he was last seen with you, in here, in the Astronomy Lab," said Hidayah.

"That's right. He was explaining the secrets a rare book contained that could help the people of Baghdad. After that we stayed on into the night fixing our devices and working on our mathematics and Ishaq said he was going home."

"We never saw him again," said another brother.

"This boy, Ishaq, he is the son of the chief translator," said al-Kindi. "His main job here is to translate the books here. He is very wise and knows many secrets. Someone might have wanted his knowledge as well as the book he had."

The girls were silent, lost in thought.

"Well," al-Kindi said, with a sweeping gesture around the room, "Jannah Jewels, please feel free to explore wherever you like in Bayt-al-Hikma to help your investigation. If you need me, you can find me in the main hall. I am at your service."

The Banu Musa brothers echoed al-Kindi's words of service, and the Jannah Jewels thanked them. They went to a workbench in a far corner of the observatory to plot their next steps.

Sara whispered "Why would someone want to kidnap Ishaq?" asked Sara. "Just because of a book? But, there are so many valuable books in here."

"Don't you remember the manuscript we found at Timbuktu?" said Iman. "It was like finding treasure! This book is the same!"

Iman explained: "Just like Timbuktu was, in the 9th century, Baghdad was the centre of learning of the world. This city attracted scientists, philosophers, writers and artists from all over the world, and produced great discoveries that changed the way people understood the universe, and the rules God has created for how it

35

functions. Scholars, writers, authors, artists, translators, scientists and inventors all gathered together in the House of Wisdom. They discovered many of the concepts we take for granted today. You know the numbers we use today - like 1, 2, 3, 4 - well, they were introduced to the world by al-Kindi!"

"Many people want to have the knowledge of the world and they will stop at nothing to get it. Knowledge is a sign of power and these books are indeed powerful, if not, transforming, just like in Timbuktu," said Hidayah, getting up from the workbench slowly. She was thinking both of Ishaq and of the pen they needed to find. She wondered if there could be any connection between the two.

Hidayah decided to pray.

"Please our Lord, help us find Ishaq *and* the missing artifact!" she said with her heart.

Hidayah spoke to the other girls: "Okay Jannah Jewels, we need to keep our eyes peeled for clues as to Ishaq's whereabouts *and* be on the lookout for any pen that resembles the one on the map!"

Hidayah walked in between the telescopes and

workbenches that dotted the observatory floor, still lost in thought. Suddenly, she caught sight of two pairs of eyes partially hidden by a large map of the stars that hung in one corner of the observatory. As soon as they met with hers, the eyes quickly disappeared. Whoever these eyes belonged to must have heard the conversation the Jannah Jewels had with al-Kindi and the Banu Musa brothers!

Hidayah, her heart beating quickly, took a few steps towards where the watchers were. But when she got close, she discovered they had gone!

Hidayah went back to the rest of the Jannah Jewels and described what had happened. None of the girls was quite sure what do to next. Suddenly, Hidayah felt the answer to her prayers forming in her heart. It was telling her to go outside.

"Come on girls, I have a feeling we need to move quickly," said Hidayah. Jaide took the lead in guiding the girls out of the House of Knowledge and back into the sunlight.

As they stepped out from the House of Wisdom and back into the sunshine, the Jannah Jewels were bumped from behind and almost pushed to the ground by two men who then ran past them and down the street in front of them.

Sara started to run after them, and the rest of the Jannah Jewels followed her lead.

After running for quite sometime through the twisting streets of Baghdad, the Jannah Jewels lost sight of the men. The girls were left standing in the middle of a large marketplace with hundreds of people walking, talking and shopping all around them. As they caught their breath, Hidayah had a chance to confirm Sara's suspicions, explaining that there had been two watchers with them in the observatory, and they were likely the same two men they had been chasing.

5

Moe And Slim

The Jannah Jewels wandered the marketplace, walking up and down, looking at stalls with books, paper, pens, paintings, clothes and food. They saw many beautiful pens, but none with a ball shape at its top. All the pens were long and slim and were the same shape from their tip to their top. After examining the pens at five different stalls, the girls were starting to feel stumped.

Jaide drooled every time she passed by a foodstall. She asked several stallkeepers for a free sample.

"You only ask for a sample with the intention that if you like it, you'll buy it from them," said Sara.

"Well, I haven't decided which stall I want to buy

from yet, so I figure I might as well sample as much as I can first," said Jaide with a smile.

CRASH!

Large wooden shelves of a nearby stall came tumbling to the ground. Scrolls, bottles of ink, sheets of paper, and pens big and small went flying into the air.

"No, no, no! Not the paper," cried the stall keeper. "Don't you know how precious these pieces of paper are?!" The stallkeeper was a large man with a small red cap on his head. He had ink all over his fingers. He looked like a hardworking man.

"Paper is precious, precious I tell you! Paper is the reason why we have knowledge and the House of Wisdom," the stallkeeper cried out, looking in dismay at the spilled ink and pieces of paper lying all over the street.

"I know very well the precious-ness of paper, you don't need to give me a lecture about it," said a familar gruff voice.

"It's Jaffar!" cried Sara. "Quick, over there!" The girls ducked behind a stall of sweet-smelling oranges, a distance away but still close enough to hear what was happening.

"What's he doing in the same time and place as us, again?!" whispered Jaide.

"He keeps finding us because he has a duplicate map!" Iman whispered back. "Do you remember what Sensei said about Jaffar's time travel?"

"I remember. Jaffar's father hired a scientist to build a time-travel machine. As you know, only children can time-travel, that's why Jaffar has to go on the missions and not his father," explained Hidayah.

The girls peered over the boxes in front of them to see what Jaffer was doing. It was clear from his angry attitude that he had been the one to bring the pens and paper crashing down from the stall. Now he was rummaging roughly through the pens, pointing at the picture on the ancient map and demanding the stallkeeper give him the same pen. The stallkeeper kept shaking his head back and forth, clearly still angry from the disarray at his stall. He started picking up papers off the ground and brushing the dust off them. A small group of people gathered around to help him.

All of a sudden, Jaffar picked up the stallkeeper by

his shirt, even though the stallkeeper was twice his size, and lifted him into the air. The old man's sandals came off his feet as he dangled in the air like a fly in a spider's web. The stallkeeper was brave. He did not even plead or beg to be let go, but instead just stared at Jaffar.

"I don't know what you want," he said firmly. "I don't have this pen you seek."

Finally, Jaffar let go. The paper stallkeeper fell to the ground and blood gushed from his knee. Jaffar kicked the stall and angrily marched away, a flurry of papers floating behind him. His two friends, Moe and Slim followed close behind spitting orange seeds to their sides as they walked along.

"At least I ask for a sample of food," said Jaide. "Not like these two goons."

"Moe, Slim, let's go!" said Jaffar. "Quit fooling around."

Moe was short with a very round belly and had a lot of very curly hair on his head. Slim was very tall and thin, like a straw. Moe and Slim were Jaffar's friends. They all went to the same dojo and learned archery together.

The Jannah Jewels crouched lower as the trio passed the orange stand. Jaide stuck out her leg as Slim walked by.

WHOOSH!

Slim fell headfirst into a large bucket of ice with fish. He jumped back, his face and hair dripping wet and punched Moe in the shoulder.

"Hey, what's the big idea, Slim?" said Moe pushing him back hard. "I didn't do anything."

Then Slim, smelling of fish, pushed Moe back. And back and forth they went, yelling and pushing each other. Jaide giggled behind the orange stand.

All of a sudden, Jaffar turned around and stared at Moe and Slim with angry red eyes. Moe and Slim stood up straight, all the blood draining from their faces.

"Go check on our little friend," roared Jaffar. "I'll be back in the warehouse in a short while."

Moe and Slim hurried away. Jaffar walked further and then seemed to head towards a man selling mint tea at a stall. Jaffer pulled the man off his stool and sat down in his place. He helped himself to tea, spilling most of it all around the table. The tea seller stood cowering nearby, clearly frightened by Jaffar. Jaffer gave him a menacing look and then reached into his pocket, took out a pen and paper and began scribbling something.

"Take this to the House of Wisdom immediately," said Jaffar to the frightened tea-seller who nodded his head rapidly and ran down the street towards the House of Wisdom. The girls watched as Jaffar sat there drinking the rest of his tea.

Jaffar seems even angrier now than last time, thought Hidayah.

Hidayah felt a cold shiver race down her spine. Her heart started beating faster and her palms became sweaty as she watched Jaffar. Jaffar seemed lost in thought.

Jaffar ran to the bridge. He was six years old. Jaffar and Jasmin met above the mighty river. Across the river, they set up a chair with an apple balancing on the top of it. They walked over to the other side of the bridge. Jaffar went first and he missed the apple by just an inch, as the arrow landed in the chair and made the apple fall to the ground. Moe picked it up and balanced it back on the chair. Then, Jasmin readied her bow and arrow. The intensity of her eyes held the object for a short while and then she shot the arrow. She split the apple exactly down the middle and it fell over into two identical halves. Jaffar looked at Jasmin and congratulated her. But Jaffar's mother who had been, all the while, standing nearby and observing the scene, would never forget the look on Jaffar's face. It was a look of defeat and anger.

"You lost to a girl!" said Moe.

"Way to go, Jasmin," said Slim, chewing on one half of the apple.

Jaffar ignored Jasmin after her victory. He said that Father had him doing a lot of extra training on his own and couldn't play anymore. Jasmin didn't understand what the problem was. She was just having fun. Jaffar kept Jasmin out of the games everybody would play together and slowly a wedge appeared between them. Khan explained to Jasmin that Jaffar was upset that he was not matching up to her skills as a talented archer and that he had put a lot of pressure on his son to excel before the Master Archer was to pick the next heir to the throne. Jasmin thought their brother-sister bond was *more important than winning some silly tournament. But, since that day, Jaffar was never the same again and Jasmin would always remember it.*

Suddenly, Jaffar got up and threw the stool he had been sitting on against the wall. He ran down the main street of the marketplace after Moe and Slim, his bow and arrow looming behind him.

Hidayah clenched her fist so tight that her knuckles turned white. She felt something gnawing inside of her. It was anger, too. She didn't feel that sorry for Jaffar anymore, especially now that he was hurting innocent civilians.

I will not let you go, next time I see you Jaffar. Enough is enough! thought Hidayah.

"I will go after them; you three go back to the House of Wisdom and figure out what is in that letter. You must warn al-Kindi and the Banu Musa Brothers," said Hidayah.

6

Checkmate

Iman, Sara and Jaide raced behind the mint tea seller back to the House of Wisdom. They finally arrived, out of breath, and found al-Kindi with a team of his students, organizing a caravan to deliver food to some of the needy families outside of the city that evening. The Banu Musa Brothers were on hand and helping as well. The mint tea seller came in and handed the letter to al-Kindi.

Al-Kindi's eyebrows scrunched up and he pulled at his beard as he read the note. Then he handed it to Iman. It was in Arabic. Iman translated it to English and read:

I have Ishaq, the son of the chief translator. If you

ever want to see him again, you must deliver the ball-tipped pen to me at once or you will never see Ishaq again.

* * *

Moe and Slim arrived back at the warehouse where Jaffar had said he'd meet them.

"I think we lost her," said Moe.

"Let's get up the stairs and see our little friend," said Slim.

Hidayah slipped in right behind Moe and Slim and hid in the shadows. As her eyes adjusted, she saw that the warehouse was full of cages of pigeons.

They must be messenger pigeons, thought Hidayah.

Moe sauntered over to a corner of the room, where a young man was sitting tied up in a chair with a lock. He was wearing long robes and a turban like those of the people of knowledge. He wriggled around trying to get loose. Moe said something to him in a low whisper, and Hidayah caught the name: Ishaq!

Moe seemed to have told Ishaq to be still, for the boy stopped moving around. Moe, acting as a guard, sat himself down near the boy's chair. After a while, Moe seemed to relax, putting his head against the wall as he waited for Jaffar.

Slim was on the other side of the warehouse peering in the cages, cooing and feeding the pigeons. The room was filled with the soft rumblings of these grey and white birds. Time seemed to pass quickly and soon Moe had fallen asleep where he sat. Slim kept looking through all the boxes. Hidayah's intense eyes searched the room as her mind searched for what she should do in this situation. As she moved to a different hiding spot to get a better view of the room, she noticed something sparkling in the darkness. Hanging on a long chain from Moe's front shirt pocket were keys! As soon as Slim's back was turned, Hidayah tiptoed across the warehouse. Ishaq's eyes widened as he saw Hidayah. Hidayah held up her finger, signalling him to be quiet. She crept up to Moe who was now snoring as loud as a gorilla. It grew eerily darker in the tiny room. Suddenly, Slim called out to Moe. Hidayah hid behind a big box.

"Moe? Hey, who's there?" asked Slim.

Moe scratched his head and turned it to the other

side. Hidayah used the end of her arrow to slowly pull the keys out of Moe's pocket. Slim got up from his chair, putting a pigeon back into a cage.

Slowly, slowly... Yes! Hidayah did it!

Loud footsteps were coming closer. Hidayah raced to the back of the room and hid behind a large table with a chess game on it. She tried to control her breathing. She felt tiny legs crawl over her arm as she lay flat across the wall trying to blend in. She could also feel them on her face. Hidayah didn't like the creepy crawly feeling of the bugs because she was very afraid of spiders. She batted at them and then hit the table by accident sending the table, the chess game and the chess pieces to the floor.

"Somebody is in here with us," said Slim shaking. "Maybe it's a gh-gh-ghost!"

"It's not a gh-gh-ghost – aaah!" said Jaffar.

Jaffar entered the room and nudged Moe sharply with his foot. "Gimme the keys."

"Hey, what's the big idea, Slim – oh – Jaffar, uh – you're back, already," stammered Moe. Moe reached into his pocket to hand over the keys, but they were gone! Moe looked at Slim and Slim looked back at Moe.

Jaffar walked closer to the table that Hidayah was hiding behind. She ducked her head away from the light and hid in the shadows. Jaffar bent down and picked up the King piece near his feet.

"Checkmate," he said as he spotted the top of Hidayah's bow in the light.

7

The Imposter

Iman, Jaide and Sara followed the trail back to the marketplace. They took turns calling out Hidayah's name.

Suddenly, a flaming arrow came crashing out a window, followed by a loud scream.

"It's Hidayah!"

The Jannah Jewels rushed toward the building of the broken window and ran up the stairs.

"Finally!" cried Hidayah. "What took you so long?"

She threw the keys high into the air to Iman. She caught it with one hand. Ishaq wriggled back and forth and then fell over to the side in his chair.

Iman reached Ishaq before Jaffar and unlocked him. All of a sudden, the large shelf that held the messenger pigeons came crashing to the ground and all of the pigeons came flying out of the cages in a huge flutter. Pigeons flew this way and that. When the fluttering stopped and the last pigeon flew out of the window, Hidayah and Ishaq had disappeared!

"Hidayah!" cried Jaide.

Sara and Jaide started throwing boxes at Moe and Slim. Iman ran to the window just in time to see Jaffar grab an old man out of his horse carriage. He threw Ishaq and Hidayah into the back. They were trapped!

* * *

Hidayah finally stirred awake. Her head was throbbing. She heard voices but they all sounded far away. Hidayah's breathing was quick and uneven. As she looked around, she realized that she was by herself in a room. She could see Jaffar through a small window talking to some people. Jaffar was strangely dressed in elegant robes with a stylish turban and had groomed his face and hair. She kept staring at the growing crowd, when all of a sudden, Jaffar turned around and Hidayah saw that he was talking to al-Kindi! Hidayah was back in the House of Wisdom.

Dazed, she could see that people were walking toward her. Hidayah looked anxiously at al-Kindi and stood up drowsily.

"This is Prince Omar. He found you in a burning messenger pigeon warehouse. He said he heard you from outside, coughing and choking. So, he rescued you and then brought you here," said al-Kindi. "I believe we owe him much gratitude for his heroic actions!"

"Assalamu alaykum," said Jaffar in the kindest way.

Hidayah thought she was going to be sick. She held her head in her hands. The room was spinning and her stomach felt like it was burning.

"How are you feeling?" asked al-Kindi.

Hidayah threw up all over the floor right in front of Jaffar and al-Kindi.

"This is not a Prince..." said Hidayah.

"Hidayah! You bumped your head. You are not making any sense right now. Omar is a prince. You need to rest," said al-Kindi.

Nurses were called to take Hidayah away into another room to give her rest.

Suddenly, Iman, Jaide and Sara burst in.

"Jaffar! What's going on here?" said Jaide. They threw Moe and Slim to the ground at his feet.

"Take away your friends, Jaffar," said Jaide.

"I don't know what you are talking about," said Jaffar. "I am Prince Omar. I've never seen these men in my life. You're surely mistaken."

Moe and Slim looked astonished.

"You, you are Jaffar, the evil man who tried to kill our friend Hidayah!" cried Sara.

The Jannah Jewels took up their fighting stances. Al-Kindi looked confused. He looked at the girls and then back at Prince Omar.

"We are so sorry about this Prince Omar, I-I don't know what to say," said al-Kindi.

"Mr. al-Kindi, sir, you don't understand! He is the one that kidnapped Ishaq, he knows where he is, he still has him, he wrote the note! You have to believe us," cried Sara.

"We've already found Ishaq," said al-Kindi. "Prince Omar found him trapped in a warehouse that was on fire, along with your friend Hidayah."

"What? What is going on here? I feel like I'm in a dream. You have to believe us al-Kindi, sir," said Jaide.

Guards came and took Moe and Slim away while the Jannah Jewels were shown where to go to be reunited with Hidayah.

"I can't believe Jaffar could do this. He has tricked them, he has tricked everyone. They don't realize that he just wants the pen!" said Hidayah when she saw her friends. "He would never admit that he's looking for the pen, or they'd know he was the same one who wrote the note about Ishaq!" said Iman.

Suddenly, one of the Banu Musa brothers walked in.

"Things are not always what they seem," he said, as he was joined by his other two brothers. "We are scientists. We believe in having proof and not merely accepting conclusions handed to us. It is only al-Kindi's nobility that prevented him from applying his scientific methods on this Prince Omar. But we believed right away that there was a need to test which of two possibilities was the truth: that Prince Omar was the rescuer of Ishaq, or the actual kidnapper himself!"

The third brother spoke: "Here, let us show you how we will arrive at the correct conclusion!"

The Banu Musa Brothers were known for their talent in mathematics. Together, they had made a pen that looked almost identical to the one shown on the map. They filled the pen with real ink and clipped the front of the pen, so when anybody used it, the pen would squirt out its ink all over that person. The Jannah Jewels went back to the marketplace and found the old man from the paper stall. They told him the plan they would use to reveal Jaffar's true identity and asked for his help in doing so.

"I like this plan!" said the old man.

The Jannah Jewels walked back to the House of Wisdom. The plan was in place.

* * *

"I found it, I found the special pen!" said the paper stall-keeper, walking into the House of Wisdom. Being curious by nature, the scientists in the room came forward to see what was being shown.

The Banu Musa Brothers had copied the image shown on the map exactly.

Jaffar stepped forward from the shadows. He was still wearing his elegant robes. He looked oddly respectable in them.

"May I see the pen?" asked Jaffar. "As you all know, I am a prince from a faraway land. What you didn't know is that I must retrieve this pen for the King."

Al-Kindi looked surprised at Jaffar's revelation.

Jaffar grabbed the pen.

"At last, at last! This pen will turn my father into the rightful heir of the throne as the next Master Archer," said Jaffar.

Jaffar gazed at the pen, mesmerized by its simple beauty. He flipped it this way and that and decided to put the pen to paper. It squirted out ink all over his clothes and face covering it with black ink. He tried to get the ink off but only made it worse by rubbing it all over. Soon, his face was smeared and his eyes became big and angry.

"What is this!" he roared.

"I'll take that!" said Iman as she grabbed the pen back from Jaffar and handed it to the Banu Musa Brothers.

Jaffar took out a bow and arrow as the crowd all around gasped. He lit the end of the arrow with fire. The crowd started to run in every direction.

"Protect the manuscripts!" cried the scholars in the libraries.

"The Jannah Jewels were right about you!" cried al-Kindi. "I'm so sorry for not believing you!"

"I need this pen. Give it to me!" said Jaffar.

The Banu Musa Brothers threw the pen at Jaffar. As Jaffar caught it in his hand, more ink squirted all over his face and the pen broke in two.

"Noooooooooo!" cried Jaffar.

"We tricked you Jaffar, this isn't the real pen," said Iman. "Now, because of your anger, you have shown your real identity – not as a rescuer, but as a trouble-maker who cares only for your own goals. Look what you were willing to do to the manuscripts of this library with your flames!"

"Guards! Guards! Arrest this man!" said al-Kindi.

Before they could reach him, Jaffar was up on his feet and beyond their reach, disappearing down the long winding streets of the market place.

8

Lost in the City

Ishaq explained his long journey over brilliant green tea, courtesy of Hidayah. Ishaq ended his story by sharing how he got the valuable book, how Jaffar kidnapped him because he thought the secret treasure he carried was actually the special pen, and how the Jannah Jewels tried to save his life in the messenger pigeon warehouse.

"Thank you very much for your help, Jannah Jewels, you are right, adventure and courage have nothing to do with size," said al-Kindi.

"We have to go. Jaffar has taken a lot of time from us, already, and we still have to find the *right* pen!" cried Jaide checking her watch.

"I remember two people talking about a unique new pen when I was on my travels to find the book," said Ishaq.

"Where exactly did you hear them talking about it?" asked Iman.

"In the desert - I would go with you but I think I am needed here," said Ishaq.

"Caravans go through there on trade routes," said Hidayah. "We might find some clues there."

"Hurry, let's go, we don't have much time left," said Jaide.

The Jannah Jewels decided to do one last search of the marketplace stalls. There was a chance one of them might be carrying this special-shaped pen. They split up, with Jaide and Hidayah searching one side of the marketplace and Sara and Iman the other. Sara and Iman went down a number of narrow and winding paths. After awhile, all the paths and stalls and people started to look the same.

"I think we're walking in circles," said Sara. "Didn't we just pass by this perfume seller a few minutes ago?"

"No, he's a different perfume-seller, he's selling musk while the one down the street had rose," said Iman smelling her hands with delight.

The girls became lost. There was no telling if they were coming or going. They were quickly losing hope in finding this ancient artifact.

Just then Jaide and Hidayah turned up.

"Just in time, we were about to give up!" said Sara.

"25 minutes left girls, I don't know if I want to be stuck in this city forever, especially after what you told me about this Mongol Invasion coming up," said Jaide.

"C'mon Jaide that's not until another couple hundred years," said Sara.

Hidayah closed her eyes tight and made a special long heartfelt dua'a to Allah. After the prayer, Hidayah looked up.

"Is someone coming towards us or is it just a mirage?" asked Sara as she emptied the last few drops of water from her canteen. And, one by one, each of the girls fell down exhausted from dehydration. Thankfully, the moon was almost full, providing them with just enough light for them to see in the dark.

"Assalaaaaaaamulaykum!" said a young girl with freckles and green eyes. When she smiled, the girls could see she had a missing front tooth.

9

Gadget Girl

"Walaikum aslaam," said the Jannah Jewels.

The girl twinkled and twankled, clicked and clacked as she came over to meet the girls. She had gadgets galore in her pockets, in her belt, tied around her neck and draped over her arm. She had a compass of her own, chess pieces and a clock.

"I am Zaynab, the Gadget Girl," she said. She gave them each some water from a large container. The girls drank to their heart's content and poured water onto themselves too.

"Follow me, I will show you my wares," she said.

The girls followed close behind.

"I am the keeper of the desert. I repair things that fall

on the way and open up my market to people passing by, like you. You must come and see if you like anything."

"She has to have the pen," whispered Sara.

"Where do you get all this stuff?" asked Iman.

"I collect whatever traders lose on their way to the market place. You know, things that fall from their caravans," said Zaynab, the Gadget Girl.

"I can't run after the caravan to give things back to them," said the young girl. "By the time I discover things, the caravan is usually long gone."

Zaynab, the Gadget Girl, opened up a large mud hut as the girls gasped at what they saw. Tables, cupboards, chairs and the floor were covered with items of varying shapes, sizes, and uses.

The girls scoured the tables looking high and low, under and over.

"It looks like you are searching for something," said Zaynab with curiosity.

"No, no, just looking, very carefully," said Sara.

"Look, there in her pocket," whispered Jaide. Sure enough, it was a pen that looked just like the one from the map.

"Can I see your pen?" asked Jaide.

Zaynab removed the pen from her front pocket.

"I found it one day, as a foreign traveler rode by on his horse. He was in a great hurry. Suddenly, his horse tripped on a rock and the man lost some papers," she uncovered some papers with lines and calculations all over them, "and this pen. I actually did try to run after them but the driver didn't see me and kept going. He never came back for it. It is quite beautiful. I've never seen anything like it in the markeplace around here. If you look closely it says something on it - though I am a simple girl, and cannot read."

Iman peered at the pen where it was written: 'Sind ibn Ali.'

Excitedly, Iman cried out, "This is the famous colleague of al-Kindi, who, working with Yaqub ibn Tariq, was the first to calculate the diameter of the earth and other astronomical bodies!"

This is the pen, thought Hidayah. And, as soon as she said it, her compass seemed to twinkle in the night, as if answering yes.

"We would like your pen," said Iman.

"Oh, you would, would you? No, you don't understand, it's not for sale," said the young girl. Her big smile showed her missing tooth. "You can buy anything else in this hut, but this pen is special, and I chose it to be my own."

"But, I really like your pen," offered Jaide, scribbling down some pictures in her sketchbook of the mud hut, the room and the pen.

The girl seemed delighted by Jaide's drawing of her hut. "I like your drawings and *your* pen," she said. "I'll trade you this pen for your pen."

"No way, this is my favorite pen in the whole world," said Jaide.

"How much time do we have left?" asked Hidayah.

"Five minutes!" said Jaide.

"So how about the trade?" said Zaynab.

"My dear pen, it's been with me forever," said Jaide. "Fine, fine, fine, here!"

"Jaide, you don't have to do that," said Hidayah. "We will find another way."

"Jaide, you just told us how special and valuable this pen is to you," said Sara.

"It's okay, this is to restore balance in the world, it's just a pen," said Jaide. "Besides, I want to get out of here before the Mongols come!"

The girls traded pens. Thanking Zaynab, the girls almost flew out of the hut in their haste to get back to the tree at the top of the hill where it all began.

10

The Trick's On You

Just as the Jannah Jewels reached the bottom of the hill, they spotted Jaffar with Moe and Slim, blocking their way.

"Didn't think we would let you have all the fun," said Jaffar jumping to his feet.

Moe grabbed Jaide and kicked her skateboard away. Jaffar grabbed the pen from Jaide. Slim pushed Iman, Hidayah and Sara to the ground. Jaffar was prepared, he started to climb a nearby tree. He struck a large branch and down dropped a trap from the tree. All the girls were locked inside a large wooden crate, all except Hidayah.

She looked up at Jaffar who was holding the pen

in the air and holding onto the tree with his other hand. Then, an idea came to her. She pulled out a wrapped box from her pocket. It was a bottle of ink.

"Don't forget this!" she said. "You need the special ink to write with that pen, otherwise it's just a pen with nothing to say."

"What?" shouted Jaffar. "Give me the ink!"

Jaffar was hanging on to the tree with one hand and holding the pen with the other. Hidayah threw the box up, but she threw it up too high for Jaffar. Jaffar reached up high. All of a sudden he lost his balance with his other hand. He could only have one or the other – the pen or the ink. It all happened so quickly that Jaffar dropped the pen to grab the ink. The pen came falling down from the tree. Hidayah raced towards it, pushing Moe and Slim to the side.

"But, you can't use that pen without this!" said Jaffar. He opened the box the ink was wrapped in with his teeth.

Because he was holding it at such an angle, the ink started to spill all over him. "Nooooooo! Get them!" cried Jaffar.

Hidayah released her friends from the trap. The Jannah Jewels raced towards the time-travel tree which was so close they could see it well. There were only seconds left on the watch.

Breathless, they pushed against the tree trunk with all their strength while praying with all their heart. At last, they heard a familiar clickety-clack and the Jannah Jewels all tumbled in, disappearing into the tree.

11

Master Artist

Jaide pulled out her skateboard and down, down, down they rocketed towards the center of the tree.

"That was close," said Master Archer appearing through the dark shadows with Master Swimmer. Someone else was with them. She was wearing flowing beautiful dark green robes. It was the Master Artist. She looked just a little bit like Zaynab, Gadget Girl.

"Jaide, step forward," Master Artist said.

Jaide stepped forward, kicking up her skateboard against the wall as she approached the Master Artist.

"You showed great courage today as you were able to give up your artist pen for the artifact," said the Master Artist. "It was a test for you and you passed."

The Master Artist revealed a small handkerchief and handed it to Jaide. Jaide opened it up.

"A gift for me? Oh, you shouldn't have!" said Jaide.

Jaide's eyes opened wide in delight.

"MashaAllah! Wow! A beautiful artist pen, even better than the one I used to have!" she exclaimed. "Thank you very much."

"When you give something up for the sake of God, He will always give it back to you better than before," said Master Artist. "Good character is the true art."

Hidayah, Iman, Jaide and Sara walked over to the Golden Clock. Hidayah gave Jaide 'Sind ibn Ali's pen which they had found in Baghdad. Jaide located the three o'clock position and bent down to place the pen in place. Instantly, the pen fell into the puzzle and a light shone, illuminating the entire tree. The girls looked up to see the Masters, but they were already gone.

Hidayah thought back to Jaffar, Moe and Slim. She wondered what they would do the next time they would see her. Things were getting trickier and Jaffar seemed angrier than ever before.

"Time to go home girls," said Iman, interrupting Hidayah's thoughts.

"Yes, let's get some dinner, shall we?" said Jaide. "My mom is making her special chicken stir-fry with steamed vegetables."

"I thought you would never ask," said Hidayah.

Will Jaffar's father be mad? Will Jasmin be sent on the next mission? And will Hidayah and the Jannah Jewels find the next piece of the puzzle?

Find out in the next book of the Jannah Jewels Adventure Series: Secrets in Spain.

Don't miss the next Jannah Jewels book!

The Jannah Jewels take readers along on their most challenging adventure yet, as Hidayah and her friends travel to magnificent Spain in hopes of finding the next missing artifact.

In this book, the Jannah Jewels meet a mysterious girl in a red dress. Who exactly is this girl? Will this girl be their friend or foe? Will the Jannah Jewels find the missing artifact before Jaffar and his gang?

Find out more about the fourth book by visiting our website at

www.JannahJewels.com

Glossary

Alhamdulillahi Rabbil Alameen: "All praise is due to God" in Arabic. This prayer is said when thankful of something or to show appreciation.

Allah: It is a word that means God in Arabic.

Assalamu'alaykum: "May the peace of God be with you" in Arabic.

BismillahirRahmanirRaheem: "In the name of God, Most Gracious, Most Merciful" in Arabic. This prayer is said before beginning something one has intended.

Hadith: a saying from the Prophet Muhammad, peace and blessings be upon him

Hijab: a head-scarf or literally in Arabic it means to cover

InshaAllah: "If it is God's will" in Arabic. It is said when indicating hope for something to occur in the future.

Jannah: heaven, paradise or garden

Qur'an: The central religious text of Muslims. Muslims believe it is the word of God as revealed to Prophet Muhammad, peace and blessings be upon him, through the Arch Angel Gabriel.

Sabr: patience

SubhanAllah: "Glorious is God" in Arabic. This prayer is said when in awe of something.

Sujud: prostration, a position in the Islamic prayer where the head is lowered to the ground

Walaikum asalaam: "May the peace of God be upon you too" in Arabic and is said in response when greeted with Assalamu'alaykum

HIDAYAH

IMAN

SARA

To find out more about our other books,

go to:

www.JannahJewels.com

Made in the USA
San Bernardino, CA
17 January 2017